Penobscot Traditions
with
Little Devil Fish

PENOBSCOT
TRADITIONS
with
LITTLE
DEVIL FISH

Nicholas N. Smith

Polar Bear & Company
An imprint of the
Solon Center for Research and Publishing
Solon, Maine

Polar Bear & Company™
Solon Center for Research and Publishing
PO Box 311, Solon, ME 04979, U.S.A.
207.643.2795, polarbearandco.org, soloncenter.org

ISBN: 978-1-882190-46-1
First print edition, first printing June 2016
Library of Congress Control Number: 2016944205
First eBook edition 2015

Penobscot designs, including turtle on cover, by James Eric Francis, Sr.,
Penobscot Tribal Historian. Cover design and photo of aurora over Kennebec
Valley by Ramona du Houx.

Manufactured on durable, acid-free paper in more than one country.

To Peter L. Paul

Contents

Author's Note

This book is an attempt to show that human life in the Maine woods was possible. Today our civilization has changed, and we think in different terms. If a person gets lost in the woods, it is a catastrophe. In former times, people obtained their entire livelihood from the forest. Today our civilized fish-and-game laws do not make this possible. However, one should be able to exist, if he or she gets lost in the woods.

Along with Penobscot Indian life, I have presented some of the traditional stories and spirits. Most of these tales are almost forgotten. They were passed down by word of mouth from one generation to another. Of course, each storyteller presented the tale in a little different manner. I have tried to present them in a variation which will be understandable and interesting to the general reader.

I have lived close to the Indians for several years and learned much from them. I have eaten their food, learned some of their language, and become acquainted with many of their customs. If I tried to present a list of all those that have given me information, it would make a long list. There are many Indians in Maine and New Brunswick who hope the Indian departments will give them more understanding and a better chance in life. I shall mention only one Indian, Peter L. Paul, to whom this is dedicated. He has done much to try to further the cause of his Maliseet tribe. He has taught me a great deal of the Indian ways, encouraged me to go on with my research, and made me feel like I were one of his family.

I have tried to introduce Penobscot Native Americans realistically, before contact with the whites, as a happy, self-sufficient people. They would like to come into their own again.

1. Little Devil Fish

Young Devil Fish ate quickly and greedily of the *musqush* (muskrat). The tender, hot, brown meat from the earthen stew pot tasted good and warmed the young boy. He watched his older brother, who was gnawing on the head. From ancient custom, the person who ate the head of the musqush entertained the group with stories after the meal. This boy, a lad of sixteen, had spent the winter in the woods in the final stages of his education and had proved that he could lead a life there. The younger boy knew that the first story would be of their family heritage. Of this both took great pride, and the younger loved to hear it. This was life at its best, thought Little Devil Fish.

It was the month of April, the moon when the Indians left their winter hunting lodges and moved toward the coastal regions, where they would once again gather the salty foods. This family had been given hunting rights to Russell Pond and Stream. This ideal location, about thirty miles west of Katahdin, was a tributary of the West Branch of the Penobscot. It was not far from Mt. Kineo — the place of the arrowhead stone. A winter of abundant food put them in good spirits on this their last evening in the winter hunting camp. The story-telling would not be long tonight but would make a small boy wonder what adventures might occur on the long trip down-river to the ocean.

Soon gluttonous appetites seemed satisfied. The slow, musical voice of the adolescent began the cherished story of how their family became known as Devil Fish.

"Many, many moons ago, several boys canoed far up the Penobscot River, so far up they passed the last island. They started to fish but only caught black chub. These they kept, cut off their heads, which they put on sticks standing them up in the bow of the canoe. When this had been done, they decided to return to their village [Old Town].

"They started singing a war song, as they approached the island. Soon an old man heard them. He slipped out of his wigwam, spotted the canoe, and told the neighbors that the boys were returning with several heads of their enemies. The people came out excitedly to see, but were disappointed to find nothing but fish heads. The boys were told to stop singing so that no disaster would befall them. Modokwahando [Devil Fish], one of the boys, said to the others: 'If we return at once, our luck will be greatly improved!' This they did.

"They had gone but a short distance when they spotted a canoe approaching them. One sharp-eyed lad saw that there were two strange creatures paddling it. They were like men but had very narrow faces and very large noses, which they covered with their hands shyly. Modokwahando knew they were water nymphs. They passed close to the boys and told them that Mohawks were camped a short distance upriver.

"Devil Fish paddled silently and, seeing their camp, made camp a short distance away. After the Mohawks were asleep, the boys attacked successfully. Now they had something to be proud to stick up in the bow of their canoe. They returned to their village early in the morning singing their war song. This time they were encouraged to sing it. Modokwahando was made a great hero and allowed to found a family, which was given this hunting area and provided with food, skins for clothing, wood for bows and arrows, bark for canoes, herbs for healing, and wood for fires.

"Tomorrow we shall leave this place for our summer fishing grounds. In the fall we will be back again."

Little Devil Fish had not realized that he was tired. Now, listening to the melodious and rhythmic voice of his brother, he found that he had a hard time to keep his eyes open. He snuggled up against his father and was soon asleep.

Morning came quickly and found the family busy packing their belongings. The birch canoe, which had been placed in a tree for safe keeping during the winter, had been taken down and overhauled the day before. The ribs had been set tightly and the bark pitched where it looked weak. The young boy was going to help his father paddle this, while the more mature lad paddled the newly made moosehide craft. The skin canoe was filled with dried moose and caribou meat. In the bow were several large pieces of Kineo flint, which would act as ballast and would later on be fashioned into spear or arrow points, knives, drills, or images to be used in religious rites. Neat bundles of prepared skins tied together with cedar bark made up the rest of the load.

The birchbark lodge was left just as it was. Birchbark boxes containing the remaining dried corn, wampum, and clothing were put in the birch canoe, together with the stone tools and weapons. Before the fire was extinguished, father took his clamshell-lined birchbark box and put a large growth from a birch tree in it. This he ignited from a hot coal. This punk would give them a fire when they made camp and was probably their most precious possession.

On their way downriver, the Indians would look for fiddle-heads, the early green tops of the unfurling ferns. These would be the first fresh vegetable that the Indians had and would also act as a spring medicine. The needles of the evergreens brewed into teas gave them their necessary vitamins during the winter.

A gentle breeze blew from across the great forest, which separated them from the Mohawks, toward the great stony hill, Katahdin, which means "large hill" in the Indian language. The great wind bird, Wuchosen, must be resting after the long season of gales. The gentle lap of the water against the canoe was like music to the rhythmic motions of the paddlers. Little Devil Fish looked around him and thought of spring as something wonderful. Trees beginning to bud, robins and bluebirds arriving, the reappearance of the bear, raccoon, skunk, and woodchuck from winter months of hibernation, brave, rugged, young plants pushing their way through the earth, and the run of the smelt. All this meant spring. The red willows along the banks contrasted with the greens of the leafing bushes and trees along with the white, fluffy pussy willows. The water was high and carried them rapidly. Occasionally ice cakes floated south with them. Soon they had left Russell Pond and were in the stream, then the West Branch, and finally Chesuncook Lake.

Katahdin came to better view. The young lad looked with curiosity at the large rugged promontory, which often had its head in the clouds. Here no Indian dared to go! The deeply lined gouges, where Pamela had in all his rage started the boulders rolling down with ever-increasing speed, were clearly visible. No wonder no Indian had ever dared to ascend toward the home of the giant bird, Pamela, or the even more powerful Spirit of Katahdin!

The sun soon was in the center of the sky. The vigorous work of propelling the canoes in the spring freshet gave them good appetites. They sighted a campsite where they decided to stop for a midday meal. The father carefully took the clamshell-lined birchbark box and began a fire. Meanwhile, Little Devil Fish was picking birch buds from which they would brew a tea. While doing this, he noticed some fine, fat fiddleheads, which he stored in a birchbark box for their evening meal. The older boy fashioned a kettle from birch bark and already had the water warming when the younger lad returned.

Soon Father said that the noon repast was ready. It consisted of dried moose meat, dried corn, and hot birch-bud tea. Soon they were filled up and refreshed.

Early in the afternoon they entered Chesuncook Lake. Going was slower now. The afternoon passed uneventfully. As the sun sank lower in the sky, they came to a neck of land which stretched out almost separating Chesuncook from Caribou Lake. Here they made camp for the night.

Each pitched in to make camp. Little Devil Fish went to find more fiddleheads. It seemed to take a long time to get many. He wandered further and further away and finally spotted a large number. He picked them hurriedly, thinking how nice it would be to rest after the meal. Suddenly he thought he heard something in the water. Turning, he saw a canoe heading for the column of smoke that was their campfire. He saw that it was a Wabanaki canoe and wondered who the solitary figure might be. He raced quickly toward the campfire with his fiddleheads.

The stranger landed and greeted the older Devil Fish. The greeting was exchanged and the newcomer was invited to partake of the evening meal. Little Devil Fish shyly came into the clearing and stood behind his father, who took the greens.

The stranger had planned to camp here for the night and proceeded to set up a shelter similar to those that the older boy had erected. With his stone axe he cut a sapling and two sturdy forked sticks. He hammered the sticks into the ground and laid the sapling on them. Next he cut a large sheet of birch bark and laid it on the ground under the framework, pegging it down flat. This would keep moisture and frost from his body. Evergreen boughs were cut next—some laid on the bark and others set up against the sapling ridgepole.

During the meal, which consisted of the succulent greens and several ducks which the stranger donated, Little Devil Fish found a new friend. This man belonged to the village at Norridgewock. He told his hosts that he had made the trip to the great mountain to gather red ocher and was now on his way home. This highly prized substance was used by the Indians in their ceremonies and deposited in the graves. He also told them that he would

stop at Kineo for some of the arrowhead stone on his way to
the Kennebec.

When supper was finished, father let his fire die down and
made some cornmeal dough. This he put in the hot ashes. Then
he kindled a new fire on top of it. Little Devil Fish sat beside
the Norridgewock Indian's fire. He noticed that there was some
red-willow bark drying in front of it. This was the curing of the
Indian tobacco or *tomaway*. When his new acquaintance came
back from checking his canoe for leaks, Little Devil Fish asked
him if he needed any tomaway.

"No," was the reply. "I am preparing some for my trip home.
Do you know how we were given tobacco?"

"No," answered Little Devil Fish. "Will you tell me?"

"Long, long ago," the man began, "there was a woman who
lived among us. She was very, very good. Everyone loved her
and respected her greatly. She did lots of good among all the
Wabanaki people. She lived to be very old, perhaps as a reward
for the love of her people. One day she died. Everyone was very
sad. They mourned for her a great deal. Finally she was buried.
Three days later, the people decided to go to her grave and burn
an offering to the Great Spirit for her. When they arrived at the
grave, they found a plant had sprung up since her burial. None
of the people had ever seen it before. They decided that this
should be the burnt offering. Thy broke off a piece of the plant
and burned it. It gave off a lot of fragrant smoke. This was the
first tobacco, and the altar was the first pipe."

"Have you tired of the Kuloskap tales?" asked the storyteller. "No," came the excited reply.

"A long time ago the animals were bigger than they are now. Kuloskap made them smaller. Some he made larger. He did that to help the Indian and to make life easier for him. The moose he made smaller, so the Indian could kill him. The big beavers he drove away. [A skeleton of a nine-foot beaver was found in Eastern Canada, as well as a mastodon, which perhaps the Indians knew about.] Finally Kuloskap came to the squirrel that was as big as a bear. Kuloskap asked the squirrel what he would do if he met an Indian. Squirrel said nothing but jumped at a stump and tore it to pieces to show what he would do if he met an Indian. Kuloskap saw that squirrel was much too big. He took squirrel in his hands and stroked him. At each stroke squirrel became smaller, till he became the size he is now. Then Kuloskap saw a small animal about the size of a squirrel, which had a short tail. Kuloskap put the same question to him. The little animal made no answer but ran away as fast as he could. Kuloskap thought he would make him big like the squirrel was, because he would run away from the Indian and would do him no harm. That is why bear is so cowardly and runs at the first sight or smell of an Indian. Kuloskap made squirrel change places with bear. If he had made squirrel any larger, there would be no living in the same country with him. Squirrel is destructive enough as he is in the small form.

"Bear lost his tail when he was still small. Even then he loved fish, but being so small he could not always step into the water and get a fish as he does now. One day he was very hungry for fish and went to the water. The bank was very steep, and he looked over and saw large, beautiful fish swimming below him. He did not dare go too near the edge for fear of falling in and drowning. Lox, the cunning wolverine, came along. He saw bear sadly looking down at the water and asked what the trouble was. Bear told him that he longed for a fish. Lox thought a moment and said that if bear went out on that log, he could put his tail into the water and move it slowly with the current and a fish might bite. Then he could haul it to shore.

"Bear thought it was a good idea. He started out on the log. His tail dangled in the water. Soon he felt a sharp pain and a mighty tug. He jumped to shore. When he looked back, he found only the stump of his tail and could hear the laughter of Lox."

Little Devil Fish could not hold back sleep any longer. He went to his shelter and nestled down among the spruce boughs. He had little time to notice the flickering shadows of the firelight before he was asleep.

When Little Devil Fish woke up, he found his father already preparing breakfast. The dough which had been put in the hot ashes the night before was now a large, warm, crusty, corn cake. The Norridgewock gave the boy some maple sugar to put on his slices. As the boy ate the unexpected sweets, he was told how Miko the squirrel gave the Indians maple sugar.

"One day a young boy noticed squirrel nibbling at the ends of the maple twigs. He noticed several drops of sap run out. The squirrel licked this eagerly. The boy broke off some and tasted the sweet juice. Then he ran quickly back to his father to show him. Since then we have enjoyed the wonderful, sweet syrup and sugar of the maple."

The boy finished his breakfast and would have liked to have listened to more of the wonderful stories that this teller of tales had at his command. However, he did not wish to keep his father waiting. The next two days were quite similar—paddling, paddling, paddling. They crossed Pemadumcook Lake and entered the Penobscot. They camped on Turtle Island in the present town of Lincoln, where there were three other families. The boy looked forward to more stories.

One man greeted them and offered them a meal of smelt. The father accepted gladly. The host's family consisted of a father, mother, girl about fifteen, and a boy about eleven.

The younger boy was excited to see another lad about his own age. He soon found out that he was a member of the Quabeet or Beaver clan. During the delicious meal of smelt, these two boys became well acquainted. They ran and played eagerly together in the lengthening twilight. Suddenly Little Devil Fish motioned to Little Beaver to be quiet. Two small bear cubs were playing near the river's edge. Perhaps the hungry mother had received the aroma of smelts and thought that she could get an easy meal stealing from the Indians' camp. The boys watched for a few minutes. As the small, black, fat, furry animals continued to hit one another playfully, the boys slipped back to tell the men. No one thought that the cubs or lean mother were worth killing. They still had a quantity of bear fat, which was very valuable for cooking, as well as a remedy for sore limbs.

"We had a funny experience when we were hunting bear last winter," said Little Beaver. "We found a den and had taken a toboggan with us, so we could haul the large brute back to camp. We left the toboggan a short distance from the den. Then father proceeded to knock on the den. He called to the bear in Indian. The bear aroused himself. Soon his black woolly head appeared, then one forepaw, then the other. Father brought down his stone axe squarely in the middle of the head. I could hear the skull crack as the blow hit the soft unprotected part of the head. I helped drag the huge beast to the sled. When we got back to where we had left the toboggan, we could not find it. We could see a trail but no footprints to give an indication of who was pulling it. We followed the sled marks, and soon saw it moving. The pulling rope was up in the trees. Looking aloft, we saw Lox, sometimes referred to as Indian Devil, jumping from tree to tree and pulling the sled behind him. When Lox saw us, he dropped the harness and raced away."

The older people had finished their chores and were settling down around the campfire. The men were filling their pipes with tomaway. "Do you know the story, 'Mother of all Lakes?'" asked Big Beaver.

"No, I'd love to hear it," replied Little Devil Fish excitedly.

"Long, long ago at the pond below here [now called Cold Stream Pond in Enfield], there was a large Indian village. For some reason the Great Spirit became mad at these people. By some great natural force he caused water to flow in, and this became the first lake in the land of the Wabanaki. From it the water flowed to all other parts of our land. All the lakes received their water from it. If you could go to the bottom of the lake, you would find the village."

Little Devil Fish knew that he would have to get up early the next morning as they planned to get to the big village of Pannawambskek (Old Town.) There he would see his mother again. She had remained there for the winter to take care of her aged father.

The morning meal was quickly devoured. The corn bread did not taste quite as good without the maple syrup. As both families were going to the village, they would be good company. The Beaver family had come down from the village of Meductic on the St. John River. They had followed the Eel River to First Eel Lake and then portaged across to North Lake. They travelled to Grand Lake, where they portaged to Baskahegan River, which flows into Mattawamkeag River, which turns and twists until it reaches the Penobscot.

The great flow of water helped to carry them on their way. Once or twice Little Devil Fish heard the splashing of a moose or caribou in the water. Once he even saw a moose with its head under water looking for roots. Two bald eagles flew by. One was holding a frog in its talons. The other was attacking hoping that the frog would be dropped. A blue jay seemed to follow them. Perhaps he was looking for an easy meal after they had made camp. The day was warm, and several times he saw a fish jump after an early bug. A muskrat swam close to the bank, saw the canoes and went to shore, hiding among the early growing green bushes. Probably its home was flooded by the high water.

As Little Devil Fish took interest in all these creatures of nature, the trip did not take long. In no time they were at Olamon, another place to gather the red paint. Then the great white rocks of the northern end of his island home came into view. Soon they passed Lover's Leap — the place where the treacherous Mohawk and his traitor Penobscot wife jumped to their death, after he had been caught acting as a spy. Finally the birchbark wigwams came into view, then the landing. The canoes had been seen, and people were gathering, anxious to see who was arriving. The canoe had hardly hit the soil before the boy was bounding up the slope into his mother's arms.

Their homecoming was not all joy, however, for the lad noticed the black line of mourning on his mother's cheek. Father also noticed it, even before he got out of the canoe. As he went toward her, he motioned toward the dark line on her face.

"They buried Grandfather a week ago," she said sadly.

This man had been a great magician. When he had been a young man, he had swallowed a turtle's heart. The palpitations of a turtle's heart continue after the reptile is dead. If an Indian swallowed one while it was contracted, he would have life forever; if the heart dilates in the throat, the Indian chokes to death. This aged man had successfully swallowed the heart. He had grown extremely old and feeble. Finally he couldn't leave his bed. At times he seemed to be dead but would suddenly emit a gasp. The gasp became a hoarse wheeze. His eyes began to dry up, then the skin. Finally the eyes no longer existed — only whitened sockets. The chiefs decided it would be best to bury him, even if his heart continued to beat and he took an occasional breath. "Even though he is buried, he is still alive," sighed the woman.

Father thought that it would be best not to stay here long but continue downriver to the ocean for the salty foods. The older boy had taken a fancy to his new female acquaintance. The younger boy was showing off to the other lads of the village. This first evening was taken up with news of the winter's hunting, news of the village and speculation of the coming summer's crops and fishing. It was late when the family went to bed.

Early the next morning, father was up to begin work in the tribal cornfield. The older son went with his father but seemed to be preoccupied. Little Devil Fish went off to find his playmates. Soon he was showing off his marksmanship. He wanted to prove that he was a good hunter. He climbed into a canoe and started off for one of the neighboring islands. His friends quickly followed him. He landed and began stalking game. Suddenly he heard a strange noise — a dull scraping sound. He came to a clearing. There in front of him was a wigwam and — was it the shaggy head of a man or bear? Should he make a noise? The playmates behind him stopped also. One boy recognized the creature as Old Bear, a hunter who camped alone. The old man was surprised to see the children and called a greeting. His dog nosed them and then returned to the fire and sat down. Soon Old Bear learned why these lads were here. "Now let me tell you what happens to boys who run off in the woods," he said, continuing to scrape the fat from a freshly killed caribou hide. The young people loved this story, especially the way Old Bear told it and settled down to hear it.

"When my grandfather was a baby, his family started for a council that was to be held in Caughnawaga. They started out by canoe. At one of the longer portages, one boy's father started running along the trail with his canoe over his head. His wife came along behind carrying some of the cargo. The child tagged along by her side. He grew restless and thought that he could run ahead and find his father. The boy became lost. When she caught up with father and saw no sign of the boy, they both became very worried and retraced their steps. They still found no trace of the child.

"Instead of going on, they went back to the village and told the people what had happened. All the men decided they would go at once to search for him. No trace was found.

"During the winter, hunters kept their eyes open to discover some clue. Late in March, one person found some sharpened sticks. It might have been that the boy was spearing fish. Close by were bear tracks. Could the bears have adopted him? Still no trace was found.

"One lazy old man who had been criticized much for his idleness decided he would find the bear's den and see if the boy were there. He went and knocked at the den. The father bear came out and the man killed him. He knocked a second time and the mother bear came. She too was killed. The third time he knocked a cub came. This he killed also. Then he entered and found the boy huddled in a corner crying for those who had cared for him all during the winter. He was beginning to grow black hair and become like a bear. The man took the lad home and was received as a hero. The parents were grateful and gave him many gifts. Soon they had the boy back to his normal Indian self."

As it was close to noon the boys thought they had better start back. The mixture of strange smells seemed to urge them to remain. The drying tomaway, the skin of the caribou with its fat, bear, otter, mink, and muskrat furs on stretchers, various herbs drying on the roof of the wigwam, charred bones of the caribou and muskrat that were used by hunters to foretell the best hunting territory, moose meat drying by the fire — all this blended with the fragrance of the pine, hemlock, and spruce surrounding them.

A late spring snow squall seemed to be their answer. "We can't go back now!" they cried, appearing to be disappointed.

Their hero pointed to the freshly killed caribou and said, "I guess there is enough for all."

The broiling meat soon made the boys forget about going home. They did not realize that the sky was getting darker. The snow did not let up but came down harder. Soon it began to turn to rain. A thin jagged streak of lightning shot across the sky. The ominous silence was broken by a reverberating roar. Quickly the old timer set out an offering to the Thunder God. "If I light some tomaway for the mighty Thunder, I shall not get struck this year," reflected the hunter.

The storm was soon over, and the boys, not being able to find further excuse to remain there, started for home.

When they arrived, they noticed that some of the girls had been playing with dolls made from sprigs of pine needles. These they set on split pieces of cedar, sang a song and tapped the wood in rhythm to the music. This made the pine needles appear as though they were dancing. They might circle, clasp a partner, separate, or go by themselves. Some of the smaller children had folded thin pieces of birch bark and bitten it. After taking it from their mouths, they compared designs.

The older boy had decided that he would like to take his new-found friend for his wife. The next morning, instead of going to work, he went to her wigwam. She was sitting inside grinding some corn with her stone pestle. The bashful boy threw the large chip that he had taken with him toward her. She turned and picked it up and smiled at him. She would have him! He ran and told his father. He would now prepare to go out hunting for food for the marriage feast.

About noon he came back with a caribou over his shoulders and several partridge hanging from his belt. Early in the afternoon, the women began preparing for the feast. The savory smells from the choice Indian dishes tantalized the children. Soon the cracking of bones, the sucking of marrow, and the dogs snarling and fighting could be heard. There was enough for all.

One old man had been asked to lead the dance. Taking his turtle-shell rattle, he began a slow rhythmical beat. His voice drew the people away from the banquet. More and more people joined hands and followed him through the wavy motions similar to a snake. He began to go faster and faster until the wavy line of people was running. This was the Snake Dance, one of the dances which was used at the beginning of many of the celebrations.

When this was over they divided up into groups. The new couple was in the head group with the dance leader. All the small groups were moving in a direction opposite to that of the sun, besides doing steps of their own in the group. As the evening wore on, the dance tempo became faster and faster. At the end of each dance the word "matamalyahe" reechoed. This signified the marriage ceremony.

Although the dance lasted through the night, the young couple went to their wigwam about midnight. Early in the morning they would have to begin their trip. This would prove whether they were capable of fulfilling the duties that each would have to perform, if they were to exist. The medicine man gave them some advice, so they could remain a happy couple. After the trip, if either could prove that the other could not perform the duties, the chiefs would annul the marriage. This would be very sad because no one would want that person for a mate in the future.

As Father watched them paddle away, he looked down at Little Devil Fish and thought, "You just get them trained to be useful, and they leave you. Now I shall have to begin over again with his younger brother."

They would give them a day's start before they started for their summer camp at Bar Harbor. The young couple would go to Deer Isle.

The next morning the family started for the coast. This time all three occupants were in the birchbark canoe. Little Devil Fish realized his new responsibility — filling in for his older brother. The first test would be the falls below the village. Father picked a course and gathered as much speed as possible. Just as they were about to go over the falls, he gave a mighty twist with the paddle. The canoe was now parallel to the falls. In a split second, they were sliding down the white band of water. With another mighty twist, the man straightened the canoe, and it was once more gliding rapidly down the river. Little Devil Fish watched for rocks and logs and kept the bow of the canoe from hitting them by using his paddle to fend them off.

The trip downriver was much the same as it had been on the first leg of the journey. But now the vegetation was more advanced. Fiddleheads were easy to obtain. More birds were arriving, filling the forest with their merry voices. Once they passed an otter slide, with one of the animals about to take a dip in the water. However, he sensed the canoe and ran to a vantage point where he could see but could not be seen. The family was not in as great a hurry now. They would camp where the Salmon Pool is now located in Bangor and do some fishing, as the salmon tried to go over the falls.

They prepared camp. As they were planning to stay several

days, this was more elaborate than those made earlier in the trip. Mother began preparing some of the clay for an earthen cooking pot. After a shelter had been erected, Father showed his son how to cut and tie the bark for birchbark torches. While he was doing this, Father would make a salmon spear. This had two jaws which would prevent the fish from wriggling from the prong. He burned through a piece of rock maple and then, with a sharpened stone, split two pieces about an inch thick, by hammering the stone wedge with his axe. Then he shaped them with his stone gouge. The prong was made from hornbeam hardened by fire. The handle was a young pine that had been smothered by its taller companions. The prong was tied in, as were the jaws, with elm bark. Soon it was mealtime.

After supper, father thought of a story to tell the boy. He began: "Today you did well. We went over the large falls successfully. You were able to spot the rocks and logs, so that we did not hit and damage our canoe or perhaps even upset. Those were big jobs. Sometimes it is the smaller things that are the hardest to do. This is especially important in hunting. If you neglect the smallest detail, the animal might detect you and escape. I will tell you how a baby conquered Kuloskap.

"This happened in the days of old, when Kuloskap roamed our land. He had conquered the strongest creatures — animals, magicians, and devils. One evening he was sitting in a wigwam reflecting over his victories. He thought that there was nothing that he could not conquer. A woman sat near him. He asked her if she could think of anything that he could not conquer. She was silent for a moment, for she was a clever woman.

"'Only one,' was her reply.

"'What is that?' asked the amazed Kuloskap.

"'The mighty baby that is sitting in front of you,' she answered.

"The baby sat on the floor sucking a piece of maple sugar. Kuloskap had never married and had had few close contacts with children. He smiled at the baby and asked it to come to him. It smiled back, but made no effort to move. Kuloskap asked a second time in a much sweeter voice. The baby looked with smiling face, the sugar still in its mouth. This irritated the great man. In a loud voice he commanded the child to obey him. The seared baby burst into tears and yelled vociferously.

"Kuloskap was left to his last resort — magic. He tried all his magic spells, but still the baby sat: his tears changed to a smile. Occasionally a goo! was emitted. In despair the great man gave up, and the baby still sat sucking his sweet sugar in the sunshine, saying 'Goo! Goo!' You still find babies say goo, goo, in remembrance of their victory over Kuloskap. He was the only creature that Kuloskap was not able to conquer."

As it was dusk, father thought that it was time to start for the falls, where they could spear salmon. He took his spear and several torches. The boy carried some too. As they approached the falls, they could make out the dark forms of the fish making their way over the falls in the whitewater. They seemed to stand on their tails and then leap up through a rivulet of the falling water. If they were lucky, they landed in a small pool, where they could catch their breath before starting the next leap higher. Some almost reached the top and then were washed to the bottom by the force of the cascading water.

The Indians found a place near the bank, where they could look down and see any approaching fish. When father spotted one, the boy lit a torch so that father could judge his spearing. When he brought up a fish, the boy stuck the torch in the ground. The father turned, and the son grabbed the fish from the spear. This would be a nice change in the menu tomorrow.

Soon they had enough and started back. Little Devil Fish seemed hungry and asked his father if he could have one. As the boy had done well with his work, Father thought that it would be good for them all to enjoy a nice fresh salmon. The boy raced home to his mother who prepared the fish.

The lad split a piece of green cedar. Taking some twigs of hardwood, he cut them into wedges. The split salmon was laid on the wood and the wedges driven through and into the soft cedar. Then it was set up in front of the fire, the white wood reflecting the heat.

They smoked many of the fish, so they would have some when they got further downriver. The time seemed to pass rapidly, and before long they were again on their way downriver. The river widened. It was beautiful. The sky was blue and the water was blue. The islands and mainland were the fresh green of spring. Dogwood, cherry, and laurel were blossoming. Soon they were at the bay and camped at what is now called Castine. Other Indians were seen frequently. Here other branches of the Wabanaki Nation frequently came — the Wewenocks from further down the coast, and the Passamaquoddies from further up the coast. Seeing, meeting, and talking with these people made life interesting for them. Sometimes they hunted and fished in groups instead of as individuals. There seemed to be plenty for all.

When the family was camped near Dice's Head, Castine, Little Devil Fish heard the story of how Kuloskap killed a moose near Moosehead Lake. That place is now called Mount Kineo. Then the hunter chased the calf. At Kokadjo he threw down his kettle, that is now Kettle Mountain. He pursued the animal to Spencer Pond, where he threw down his pack. Now that is Spencer Mountain. The calf turned south, Kuloskap still after him on snowshoes. At Belfast, the pursuer jumped the Penobscot River, landing at Castine. The snowshoe marks can still be seen. Finally at St. Rosier, he was able to kill the beast. He threw the entrails to his dog. They are the white quartz, which can be seen under the water. The liver is the red quartz.

At Sedgwick they camped near the great stone bird at the Punch Bowl. Now the Indians say the white man has destroyed the head of the bird, so it does not receive much attention. In former times, it was greatly admired.

Finally they were at Pemetic — where the mountains are seen from the water in a jagged line. They camped at Oak Point and met Indians who had come down the Union River, a popular fishing resort.

Seals inhabited the islands, together with great auks. Finally they established their summer camp at Manesaydik, the clam-gathering place (Bar Harbor).

Here they gathered an abundant supply of clams, oysters, scallops, lobster, and fish. Large quantities were smoked or dried for use in the winter. They were stored in birchbark boxes. Father taught his son how to make full use of all animals. The bladder of the seal made an excellent watertight bag. The seal oil was extracted and stored in these. It was an excellent medicine. The boy learned to make tools from the bones, using his stone knife.

He became adept at throwing a harpoon at a porpoise. With his wet paddle and the sun's rays, he would signaled to a person whose luck had not been so good. The unlucky fisherman helped bring the mammal to shore, cut it into juicy steaks, broiled it, and partake. Little Devil Fish did not care too much for the greasy meat.

However, he did love a clambake. He eagerly gathered firewood and stones for these. They first made a layer of stones, then firewood, then stones, till they had a mound about four feet high. They lighted the wood. Soon this had burned down, and all the stones were red hot. Then they threw lobsters, crabs, clams, and any other seafoods that had been gathered onto the red-hot rocks, covering them with seaweed. In about an hour, they would be ready. He could hardly keep from burning himself on the hot, succulent morsels. Several times he had seen men use the larger lobster claws for a pipe.

Once in his eagerness to cut some firewood for a clambake, the axe slipped and cut a deep gash in his foot. His mother squirted several puffballs on it, which stopped the bleeding; then she took some balsam from a pine and drew the skin together and sealed it with the pitch. It was not long before his leg was as good as new.

Sometimes his mother sent him to gather the large water-lily roots. When these large, meaty, tuberous roots were baked, they were delicious. He even went to the islands and gathered auk's and gull's eggs. Sometimes he took an auk home to be roasted. He learned to read the signs left by hunters, perhaps a stick stuck in the ground pointing in a direction or a piece of birch bark marked with charcoal and stuck to a tree or bush.

He learned how to make dyes — the blue of the rotting cedar, red of the blood root, yellow of the gold thread, green of the cedar bark, brown of the hemlock. He liked to go berrying but liked to eat them much better than to use them for dyes.

Soon summer would be over and the beauty and good times of Bar Harbor a dream until another year. This was life at its best for the lad. It was a life of continual hunting and fishing for survival. It was a life of nature — animals, plants, birds, fish and stones. It was a life of beauty — a delicate flower, a young moose, or a magnificent day. It meant a continuous cycle of moving. All this was what the Indian lived for and what kept the Indian living.

One evening young Devil Fish asked his father if he had ever seen Kuloskap; "No," replied the adult. "The great master is living still, but no ones knows where. He may be to the north, to the east, to the west, or to the south. If you have faith enough and go and seek him, you will find him. They say he is in a great wigwam. He is making arrows there. When he has the wigwam filled, he will make war on all the world and kill all living things. That will be the end of the world. Perhaps some will be saved; perhaps everything will be destroyed. Perhaps the end will be tomorrow; perhaps not for a generation. It is good not to know all what might happen. We can go on living just as we are, thinking of tomorrow and all that we must do to keep our families happy. If we live well, perhaps the great Kuloskap will see and change his mind or wait until we have passed into the Happy Hunting Ground before he works his powers of destruction."

The sun was rising behind the trees wearing a pale gray veil as if bashful to show its full face. Dim shafts of it's pale, golden, mellow light peeked through the dark forest's trees and brush here and there, opening the forest for another day where bands of bird families were already actively gathering. Late summer showers were beginning to replenish the rivers and streams from summer lows, making them again fine arteries for transportation. These were necessary factors that preceded Wabanaki preparations for winter. They, like the birds, would soon be migrating for winter habitats.

Mother stood straight and tall after finishing her breakfast of bannock and fish. There was a reddish image of a fish on her lower left arm. Her mother had told her many times of when she was pregnant with her and very hungry, when she saw one of the men walking to his wigwam carrying a beautiful salmon. How her mouth watered for the fat, nutritious fish! She was too bashful to ask the fisherman for even a small piece of it. All day she focused on her desire for that fish, and that night she dreamed about it. When her daughter was born several weeks later, there was the red image of the fish embellished on her tan arm. It remained there for the rest of her life, acknowledging her mother's desire for the fleshy fish.

Then she began preparations to take the children to harvest the fine crop of blueberries. The children were happy thinking about picking the succulent berries that were used in so many ways to add flavor to many foods that they enjoyed. Mother was gathering together birchbark baskets of various sizes. The youngest children would have the satisfaction of filling their own basket and dumping it into a larger one. The older children looked after the younger ones, and soon they were ready to proceed to the blueberry barrens about a mile away. The mother led the group; the children followed like a covey of grouse moving sporadically to investigate something to the left or right, sometimes stopping, then running to catch up. At times they stopped to pick tea berries in the rich ragged rocky forest turf. The berries left a refreshing flavor in their mouth that lasted for some time. There was a large rock with almost sheer sides that was always a challenge for young children to climb. Each child had to reach the top or attempt to do so. Then they ran to catch up to Mother.

They finally reached the blueberry barren; a few leaves had already begun the change to their fall-red coat that would soon turn the entire barren to brilliant scarlet. Mother scanned the bushes. It was not unusual to see a bear or two lunching on the berries and spitting out the unwanted leaves. There was enough for all. A few times she had seen a mother with one or two cubs with ravenous appetites enjoying a visit to the barrens. She always gave bear families a wide berth. As she surveyed the large expanse of blueberries, she recalled a tradition told by one of the popular elders, noted for his creative stories. She reviewed the yarn in her mind smiling at parts.

A young hunter was crossing the barrens at blueberry harvesting time. He had gone about a half a mile, when he came upon a large expanse of bushes that apparently had been ignored by man and beast, except a few birds. Before starting to fill his basket, he turned and looked behind him. He saw a figure in the distance. Assuming that he was looking for blueberries, he beckoned him to come. He started picking. They were some of the biggest berries he had ever seen. He looked to see if the figure behind was getting closer. He still looked very far off, so he beckoned with his hand and arm again. Then he continued picking. It was not long before he heard footsteps behind him. He turned to greet his companion. To his great surprise it was a bear! The bear seemed to be contented to find a spot by himself to enjoy the berries. Neither bear or man disturbed the other. Each knew that there was plenty for all.

The berries were of high quality, and most were very large, many the size of the hunter's thumbnail. Soon his basket was filled. He attached a cedar-bark rope to form a tumpline that would go around his forehead, supporting the weight of the basket that sat on his back.

The following fall, the hunter was hiking through the blueberry barrens to a place noted for wild cranberries. He also hoped to come upon a fat deer. He saw a figure far a head of him that turned and beckoned him on. He walked faster wondering who he was. His friend had stopped but kept on beckoning him. The hunter went as fast as he could on the rough ground to catch up. As he approached closer, he saw that his friend was the bear who had followed him on the blueberry barrens earlier.

The bear waited for the hunter. Not far from them several deer grazed on the grasses and foliage. The hunter swiftly fitted an arrow to his bow, thanked the deer for allowing him to kill it, and shot a fine fat young buck. He turned to thank the bear, but it had already silently vanished, making his way through the thick growth. It was good to be kind to all the forest creatures.

Mother stopped and surveyed the area but saw only a few birds here and there pecking at the berries. She said to herself, "There is plenty for all," as she put her baskets down. When the children approached she gave each one a birchbark basket to fill. The largest ones were handed to the older children, the smaller ones to the younger. The children went off, each one wanting to be the first to fill his or her basket. The older children finished first. Mother sent them to fetch some dead, dried wood, so she could make a fire to heat tea and bannock. She had put lumps of fat that melted in the bannock when heated and was absorbed through the bread, making the cold, tough, brittle breads softer, warmer and more palatable. After the meal Mother and the older children fitted their baskets with a tumpline and started home with their baskets on their backs.

That night, supper included bannock laced with blueberries, as well as stewed blueberries. As the sun set, sending brilliant, scarlet rays across the sky, all nature's signs pointed to a bright sunny day for the morrow. Mother's plan was to stretch out sheets of birchbark flat on the ground and spread the blueberries over them to dry in the sun. When the berries were dried, they would be stored in birchbark containers, to be used as a condiment or spread for many meats and fish. The treat that most people considered to be the best was dried blueberries mixed with thickened maple syrup, as a spread on moose meat. It was not only their favorite meal but often served on special occasions.

It was getting near the time for leaving the coast and starting for winter quarters, before snow began to fly. There would be plenty of work for all to do in preparing for the annual move. They always saw several old friends along the way. After greetings, there would be an exchange of news. People passed the news from the different parts of their hunting districts. Most people were fairly well informed of any unusual events that happened in their land.

2. On the Move

The seasonal moves were a well-established routine. When one considers the large Indian population that roamed Maine's North Woods, the archaeologists have to acknowledge that the footprints left behind on the land are rather small and well covered. Indian land-use methods caused only slight disturbance to the terrain. They moved periodically, yet left little trace of where they camped. They became a canoe-people, adapting to the marvelous waterways for highways, as much at home on the water as the ducks that flew up after the canoes rounded almost every river bend. This means of transportation demanded very slight maintenance but led them to their best food sources. All game relied on water and on the plants that grew in the water or along the riverbanks.

When traveling, it was the custom to sleep under an overturned canoe; sometimes the shelter was enlarged by attaching a roll of birchbark or skins from the canoe as far as they extended. Older boys and young men often preferred to sleep under the stars and watched the planets and shooting stars move across the heavens. The North Star or constellations like the Hunter chasing the Great Bear were their guides at night. The Hunter always caught up to the Great Bear and killed it at the end of summer. The Great Bear's blood dripped down sprinkling the leaves of trees and shrubs, turning them red.

It was dusk. Mother noted that the days were becoming shorter. She hardly looked up from the moose-shank boot that she was making, when Father entered the wigwam. He turned his attention to the his youngest son, resting in the cradle-board leaning against the side of the shelter. The cradle was like a home within the home, for the parents knew that their son was safe in it. Otherwise he might wander to the hot fire and get burned, sneak outside and get lost, or touch the hot water in a birchbark kettle and get scalded. Mother carried him on her back when she was working outside and might even hang him on the limb of a tree, so she could work unhindered but could always watch him, while she moved among the varieties of berry bushes.

There was a flutter at the door and a low rattling sound. It was not enough to get the attention of the wigwam's inhabitants. A few minutes later, there was a more vigorous shaking of the door flap. Then a scratching at the door flap, followed by a more vigorous shaking. The creature emitted a low guttural sound. All those inside immediately turned to the door. The younger children moved to the back of the wigwam. Father moved quickly to the door as he picked up a stone hammer. The head of a bear protruded through the flap in the half-light of the shelter. The creature, knowing that he was now the center of attention, began in a low sonorous tone turning into a fast cadence that rose quickly, "hi yah, hi yah, hi yah." Everyone was attentive and quiet. The bent-over masked singer began a riddle in his melodic, poetic language, translated here.

> This is the reason I'm here, my friend.
> I brought this trading article, my friend.
> Return article is what I want, my friend.
> Now bring something to me I need.
> For this is just what you need, my friend.
> Now if you like this article of mine, my friend,
> Bring to me the return article, my friend.
> Now if you cannot come with it, let me know.
> Of course the evening is long, my friend.
> Don't think that you can outdo me.
> There is a lot of this stuff, where this came from, my friend.
> Don't think that you can get the best of me.

So attend to this right away, my friend.
It is hard going, the snow is getting deeper, my friend.
I think that this has come to stay, my friend.
It's a bad hail storm, my friend.
Don't think that I can't walk through it; I have snowshoes too, my friend.
I will snowshoe over; now it's whatever you think, my friend.

The children looked at one another and then at their parents. "That is Uncle Horace again," said Mother. "He is always the first one to leave for his winter camping place, so he's the first to perform the Trading Dance."

The Trading Dance is a single performer who moves jerkingly as he sings his riddle explaining what he has to trade. It was more of a game than a dance. Mother asked the children, "What do you think he has to trade?"

The children looked puzzled. The younger ones looked up to the older ones for an answer. One replied, "food!" Another, "Rabbit skins?" A young child in an outburst chimed in, "Porcupine quills?"

Father began, "The riddle that Uncle Horace sang implied that his trade article is something that we need and that he has plenty of it. I know he killed a bear the other day that had a thick layer of fat. Several days before that he killed a fat raccoon. My guess is that he has an abundance of fat stored in a birch container. Now I have to get ready to return his trading visit and take that handy small stone chisel. He will have many uses for it during the winter.

"Uncle Horace winters far to the north, where there is a great variety of animals to harvest for their meat as well as skins to fashion into warm clothing, bags, and other necessities. He knows his land well and the animals it attracts and produces. He has a fine reputation as a hunter and has trained his boys well to take their places as respected providers in our tribe." The solitary life of the hunters forced the people to have many skills. They had to rely on themselves for all necessities.

Father found a medium-size stone chisel to exchange with Uncle Horace. Then he pulled out some deer skins from their supply tent to disguise himself and was off to Uncle Horaces's wigwam. He would sing and demonstrate his chisel on the wigwam poles, a paddle, or some other wooden object that he could find. His song also reminded the old hunter that it was a handy tool to open the frozen water hole in his lake in the morning, after the cold night had changed the liquid to a shiny crystal surface. It was also a fine tool to fashion skin stretchers and in the spring, shape a canoe paddle.

Versions of the ceremony were performed by most of the northern Algonquian forest hunting tribes in North America, when most the people of a tribe were about to leave for their isolated, lonely winter camps, where there were slight opportunities to visit or see others. A tool or kitchen utensil that would be used often would be a reminder, strengthening bonds between relatives and friends, who would probably not see one another until summer. Each opportunity to use these gifts acknowledged a friend's support. These ceremonies were joyful, fun social occasion, filled with humor, causing much good feeling and laughter.

When a family arrived at the mouth of a small river or stream, where one or more families were camping, the travelers were apt to spend a day or two with their friends, before continuing on their long journey. Social opportunities were limited, so they made the most of any occasion that was offered. The people knew the importance of social fellowship.

The blueberries were drying fast in the bright sun of the late summer days. Mother supervised the two older teenage girls scraping off the dried berries from the birchbark sheets into birchbark baskets, where they would be stored safely. During the harvest season, they had already picked a variety of berries, nuts, and medicinal plants, each stored in its own birchbark basket with an attractive image scraped on it with a sharp beaver tooth. The various-sized bark receptacles for blueberries, cranberries, raspberries, winter berries, acorn meal, plant medicines, and other forest products were stored in larger birchbark containers. The family was well supplied for the winter trip.

A few basic medicines, such as dried blue flag roots harvested from muddy riverbanks and the tall plant that we call cow parsnip that grows on shady moist riverbanks, both summer flowering plants, were always included. They were important remedies that no one wanted to be without. They were carefully stored in the medicine basket.

Butternuts were probably the popular nuts. A method had been learned to harvest the meats, which are still considered difficult to obtain. The nuts were smashed in wooden or stone mortars. Then hot water was poured into the mortars. The buoyant nut meats rose to the top, where they were skimmed off with a flat wooden spoon and crushed into a flour meal. Beechnuts were also a favorite.

All the small, circular bark containers were packed together in a large, round basket, making a snug fit for a safe trip to the late-fall-early-winter camp. The days spent in planing and preparing for the winter were full. Everyone knew that anything forgotten could not be replaced once they were on the trail.

The great North Woods was like a large factory or garden, the source of a great variety of animals, birds, fish, and plants to provide a varied diet. Tribal laws restricted wasteful harvesting. Children learned to be aware and concerned about conservation of all forest life that Mother Earth produced. In one way or another, it was the mix of everything in the forest that provided the needs of all life.

3. The Fall and Early Winter Camp

The days passed quickly for the busy family. The canoes selected for the trip were long twenty-two-foot birchbark craft that would carry all the people and basic materials for the winter. The long canoes had a short draft, as the rivers were lower in the fall, before the fall rainy period, than they were in the spring. They would be going upstream against the current, but the current would be much weaker than the strong, spring currents. The trip would include the entire family and all their goods needed for the long winter months. Sometimes the younger children would ride in a canoe, but when there was a flat, rocky ledge or other fairly easy walking, the youngsters walked along the shore, keeping within sight of the canoe. The children enjoyed this independence, while gaining knowledge of the river that would someday be their principal way of travel. Each day offered some different and new experiences for some of the travelers. It was all part of their education system, preparing the youth for their future. It was a real-life experience.

The experienced hunters, accompanied by the older youth of fourteen and older, were not only foraging for food but were looking for animal trails and other signs of the presence of game. It was a practical learning experience for the younger ones, while the more experienced hunters were mapping the animal activities in their brains for future reference. Late October and November snows made the tracking of animals easy. All this data was essential for these people, who depended on the forest for all their food and essentials. As the winter months passed with deepening snow, the trails would become more defined. Usually by mid February, the snowy surface froze deeper and deeper, finally supporting a hunter's weight. The much heavier animals like the moose would break through the frozen, snowy crust, making a quick getaway impossible. By mid March the snow would be up to a moose's belly, conditions that favored Indian hunters. The Indian put on his snowshoes and ran on the frozen surface after his much heavier prey that broke through into the three-foot-deep snow — almost floundering with each step.

Such were the thoughts that Mother had, as the long journey ended. Soon she would be very busy, as she had primary duties in setting up the more permanent winter camp. It would be sheltered by the tall pines of the North Woods, from the cold north winds.

4. The First Winter Camp

I t was late afternoon, but the sun was already low on the horizon. The family was happy, as they had arrived at the site of their first winter camp, a place where they were to remain for six or eight weeks. This was to be their last night spent in a rather haphazard traveling shelter.

In the morning, Mother and the older children searched for several approximately seven-and-a-half-foot-long lodge poles, gathered spruce boughs to knit as a floor, and made a stone fireplace in the center for heating as well as cooking. The children gathered firewood. The lodge poles were tied together with spruce roots. Two or three poles were tied near the top of the wigwam for strength and to provide a place where clothes, food, and medicine plants were hung to dry or warm.

First the women gathered the wigwam materials; then they set up the framework by securing saplings in the ground, bending them to the proper ovals, and then finally tying bark and skins around it. The door flaps were installed last. While the women and children were involved in making a comfortable winter home, the men left to check the familiar nearby game trails and would bring home a bountiful meal for Mother to cook.

The walls of the wigwam reflected the heat from the central fire just as they did the voices of its inhabitants. Other than conversation, there was little or no raucous noise, other than a small child's crying. Keen hearing was a basic necessity for everyone, especially the hunters. Impaired hearing was not the problem that it is in our world of almost constant, loud, sharp, and clashing sounds.

A storage structure was also necessary. The wigwam style was for living. Its space limitations did not allow for all the camp or personal gear, except what was in use. The warm skins for sleeping were either hung outside when the weather was good or placed in the storage tent on stormy days. The living quarters were open spaces, except for a kitchen area usually on one side of the door. Some foods and water were stored in the kitchen area. The back of the shelter was used for sleeping As one entered the wigwam, the parents slept in the rear center. The man's side was on the left, the woman's and small children on the right. After the bedding was cleared, the rear section became a work area.

There were several other structures making up the campsite, including a special wigwam for the hunters. It would be a rare situation that required a woman to hunt, other than setting rabbit snares, so the men had a special place for their hunting rituals. These rituals were presentations to the spirits for a successful hunt, as well as the giving of thanks for a successful hunt. The Bear Feast was the better known, but they might decide it necessary to have hunting rituals for other game, even for geese.

The goose was considered as being very special for the Northeastern Indians. The timing of the spring migration coincided with the changing season that melted snow and ice.

The melting conditions made land travel almost impossible and also created unsafe ice condition, so water travel was impossible. The regular hunting procedures had to be abandoned. Before the migration, the family moved to a site known to them that was on the migration route. The waterfowl sustained the people for about two weeks until land and water conditions permitted good traveling again.

The women also made several outdoor racks for storing meat and fish during the cold months. There was no need for artificial refrigeration. These folks loved the cold of the winter season. It was a challenge of their survival skills. There was a great variety of animals available, who found the cold to their liking. This family had learned much about hunting that had been passed down from former respected generations. The successful hunting traits of the past were the tried and tested trump cards for this family, many generations later.

Mother was up early after the first night's sleep in their new lake-side home. She went out to chop and clear the ice that had formed overnight in their waterhole. On her way she saw several Mikumwesuk, tiny people, scurrying away and hiding in the thick leaves and underbrush of the forest floor. After filling her birchbark bucket with water, she dawdled, her sharp eyes searching along the sandy shore. Suddenly she gasped with awe and excitement as she picked up two small, clay objects the Mikumwesuk had made and left for their winter neighbors. She returned to her kitchen area excitedly telling the family of seeing the little people and showing the white clay objects that were gifts from them. All this was taken as a prognostication of a successful hunting season. These findings lifted the family's spirits very high, preconditioning them for a plentiful harvest of a variety of food during cold months ahead. Mother sang a few short songs, while she happily prepared breakfast, which included a lunch of meat and Indian bread that had extra fat in it. When warmed, the hot fat melted oozing through the small round loaf, creating a warm snack for the hunters while on the trail. This would be the general morning routine for the winter months.

In February, the oldest boy was to have his twelfth birthday. It was customary to mark the first step towards manhood in the twelfth year. It was a time for the parents and the youngster to be proud of the son's accomplishment. It was the beginning, when a youth took his place in providing food for the family.

For several years, boys were trained to shoot birds with slingshots and bows and arrows. They became very proficient with these weapons. Several years before a twelfth birthday, a boy could set a row of stones on a downed tree trunk and knock them off one after another with his bow and arrow. A twelve-year-old was ready for his step into manhood.

Afterword

I accompanied Edwin Tappan Adney's best friend, the late Peter L. Paul (1902–1989), a Maliseet Indian, to Adney's cabin at Upper Woodstock, New Brunswick. We turned left off the highway, passing through a grove of tall pines that insulated the cabin from all road noise and isolated it from civilization. Then we came to the clearing. The cabin stood with its back against the pine barrier, protecting from cold north winds. It seemed like it was surrounded by the great North Woods. Although we were only three miles from town, it felt like we were miles away from civilization. It was the perfect atmosphere for one who wished to study and save the Indians' vanishing culture.

We approached the door. Peter grasped the handle firmly, turned the knob and pushed. The door had had little use for about a year and groaned under the pressure to move. The interior was light and airy, what one would expect of an artist's studio. Adney's bed was still there on one side of the one-room cabin. A large fieldstone fireplace filled most of the southern end. It was for both heating and cooking. His desk was at the north end. I tried to picture how the interior had been, with his canoe models, paintings, and at least twenty-five years of notes and correspondence that had been stored in boxes piled nearly to the ceiling.

It was a familiar scene to Peter Paul, who had worked with Adney on his linguistic studies. Paul was a younger man than the elders who usually surrounded Adney. Paul's mother and twin brother had died in the birthing process. Peter was brought up by loving grandparents, who were some of the last Maliseet living closely to the Maliseet traditional hunter's lifestyle. The hunter's language was spoken by both parents, who were born about 1860 and reared by conservative, traditional hunters born about 1820. Peter claimed that he did not know English until he was about twenty-nine.

Although Peter was much younger than the Woodstock elders, he often knew more of the language than those who spent most of their lives relying on a nearby village for life's essentials. Peter, proud of his ancestry, encouraged both young and old to speak and maintain their native language wherever he went. For him it was an essential part of being Indian.

Adney found Paul reliable, often more so than then neighboring elders. Paul was always a welcome visitor to the cabin. It did not take long for a close association to develop between them. Paul was a busy cooper and basketmaker six days of the week. A routine evolved whereby Adney walked the six miles from his cabin to Peter Paul's reservation home in lower Woodstock every Sunday. A good dinner prepared by Minnie, Paul's wife, was always ready for Adney. Dinner over the table became a work station, where Adney lit his pipe and spread out his papers, while Peter sounded off his words for Adney to capture on paper. The two worked together for fifteen years.

In 1950 I discovered Edwin Tappan Adney (1868–1950). His papers had just been deposited at the Salem, Massachusetts, Peabody Museum, where I was assigned to sort about 150 boxes of them. He had compiled his massive notes into a planned publication, *The Language of the Malecite or Etchemin Indians: Illustrating a New Method of Analysis, with Words, Sentences and Texts.* It consisted of two parts: "Part I: Basis and Principles of the Particle or Alphabetical Method of Analysis Explained and Illustrated by Indian Words, with their European Correspondences"; "Part II: Indian Words, Sentences, Texts, Classifications of Words and Ideas, Grammatical Forms Explained."

It was a massive undertaking, never completed. Adney studied the hunter's language, knowing that it was slipping away. He enjoyed ferreting out the old hunters, people who had become silent onlookers of the culture that was replacing theirs. Adney learned as much of their language as he could and was soon thinking and speaking Maliseet.

It was a very precise, organized work, establishing rules of grammar, of pronunciation, and an alphabet based on letters from the English language to produced the proper Maliseet sounds.

The work established the forms for writing the language, using the familiar English alphabet. The old language was the heart of Maliseet culture and their philosophy of life, the life of survival in the North Woods. The words were descriptive nouns of people's names, their actions, place-names, animals, plants, etc. A few bird and animal names were imitations of their calls. By adding prefixes and suffixes to the descriptive name for deer, as an example, one knew that the animal referred to was an adult or fawn, male or doe, and if it was alone or accompanied by others. One word described it all.

If the people were forced to delete hunting from their lifestyle, their language would be destroyed. A new language would replace the hunter's language. The language of whatever type of life replaced hunting would include many new words, as well as some from the old vocabulary, but remolded to fit new situations. However, the transcribed meaning of the old words might seem the same, because they described similar action but the transcribed action fitting the new situation was usually different. Such words can be compared to an old diamond ring that has been placed in a new setting, giving it an entirely different appearance.

Adney started with common everyday expressions, verb forms, pronouns, and moved into the complex terms of the natural world: names of months, place-names, geographic terms, expanding to names for canoe parts and canoe tools, traditions, and customs. The papers reflected Adney's broad interest in all aspects of Maliseet Indian life, the local Indians of the St. John River Valley of New Brunswick.

His work was not only the saving of a language, it was the saving of a culture, for here are words necessary for the traditional trappers and hunters to supply the families with sustenance, the skins that clothed them, and all the forest products for their hardy livelihood. He learned that nouns were animate or inanimate, that material like strong straight limbs or boards included a suffix expressing that quality, while those that were flexible like rope were expressed by a different suffix. Wind directions were expressed from describing the terrain from the direction they came. Whereas the winds from the four directions seem so easily expressed in English as north, east, south or west, they became different for each Maliseet village or camp location. North might be "from the mountains and forests" at one camp, while "from the lake and hills" or "upriver direction" or "downriver wind" at others. The wind directions were also a method of stating a camp's location.

In the mid twentieth century, there was a new breed of professional linguist. Harvard Professor Karl Teeter came to the St. John River searching for Peter Paul, with an introduction that Adney's system of linguistics was outdated and inadequate. He would like to introduce Peter to the new system and work with him. He could also pay Peter Paul to work with him from a Canadian Museum of Civilizations grant. Neither Adney nor could I afford the luxury of paying Peter.

The new system of linguistics came with a new vocabulary based on twentieth-century American life. C. Douglas Ellis, a linguist of the Cree language, a neighboring dialect, created a course with tapes for those who wished to learn Cree. As Cree was very similar to Maliseet, I played the beginning tape to Peter Paul. It began with "Good morning." Peter broke in, "Stop! That ain't Indian. That's English. He is using an English greeting. We never used one like that. He uses the Indian word for 'good' and 'day.' We never spoke like that." The tape went, "What did you have for breakfast? Oranges, cereal, and toast." Pete continued, "We never had oranges, cereal or toast."

The Maliseet had two traditional greetings. The first was

to those one saw frequently and knew well, extended family members, a simple "Kwey." The second was to those one sees after a period of absence, after he has resettled into the community. It was a much longer word that enquired about his health and welfare during his winter hunting, generally a period of four or five months.

Several yeas ago, some Passamaquoddy elders interested in preserving their language asked if I would give them a copy of a tape of Peter Paul's vocabulary. I did. The elders responded by saying about some words, "That's the way we spoke when we were young. Now these professors give us a different way of saying it."

I'm sure that as the culture changed, the people would have created new terms to reflect the changes in their lifestyle, if they had been given the opportunity. The new linguists introduced not only a new language but a new culture quite foreign to the traditional life the people had enjoyed.

Adney's work is important, for it defines the traditional way of Maliseet life, just as the vocabularies compiled by the early missionaries do.

The Author

Nicholas N. Smith was born in Malden, MA in 1926. After serving in the 9th Air Force in Europe during WWII, he received his B.A. in history from the University of Maine and a Library of Science degree from Columbia University. His advisor at UM suggested that he study Maine Indian history. His research in this fascinating subject has taken him to many university and special libraries in the U.S., Canada, England, and Germany. He is the author of many papers concerning the Wabanaki and the Cree of Lake Mistassini in Northern Quebec and received an honorary doctorate from the University of Maine in 2007. The author and his wife, Edyth, live in Brunswick, Maine.

www.ingramcontent.com/pod-product-compliance
Lightning Source LLC
Chambersburg PA
CBHW050320200626

46812CB00019BA/2944